D0189351

This Little Tiger
book belongs to:

For Freddie and Matilda, with love
~ M C B

For Coral Bahrani
~ T M

LITTLE TIGER PRESS
1 The Coda Centre, 189 Munster Road, London SW6 6AW
www.littletiger.co.uk

First published in Great Britain 2012
This edition published 2013

A CIP catalogue record for this book is available from the British Library

 • ISBN 978-1-84895-484-7

Printed in China • LTP/1800/0571/0613

2 4 6 8 10 9 7 5 3 1

One Starry Night

M Christina Butler   Tina Macnaughton

LITTLE TIGER PRESS
London

One clear, bright night, Little Hedgehog saw a shower of shooting stars sparkle and flash across the sky.

"Wow!" he gasped. "I must tell everyone!" And off he ran.

"Have you seen the shooting stars?" Little Hedgehog called out, as Fox and Mouse walked home through the meadow.

"I've seen three!" cried Rabbit, hopping up.

"Can we stay up to watch them, please?" squeaked the baby mice.

"All right," said Mouse. "And let's get Badger, so we can all see them together."

They rushed into the wood, but a huge tree had fallen across the path.

"We can't get over that!" Little Hedgehog cried.

"I can," said Rabbit, scrambling on to the tree. "Give me a hand, Fox."

So Fox pushed
and Rabbit pulled
until everyone was
over the other side.

Puffing and giggling they arrived at Badger's house.

"What's all this?" he said.

"Shooting stars, Badger!" cried Little Hedgehog. "Come and see!"

"There are hundreds and hundreds!" squeaked the mice.

"Wonderful!" said Badger. "Let's go to the top of the hill. We'll see them better from there."

As they marched on, the babies began to sing: "*Twinkle, twinkle, little star!*"

"*How we wonder what you are!*" joined in Badger.

"*Shining brightly, flashing by,*
Like a sparkler in the sky!" laughed Fox.

"I'm going to catch a shooting star!"
Rabbit called out, racing ahead.
Higher and higher he
jumped when suddenly . . .

he fell down an
old badger sett!
"Rabbit!" yelled
Little Hedgehog, and
they all raced to help.

But as they peered into the hole, the sides crumbled and everyone tumbled in . . .
BUMPETY, BUMP! CRASH!

"Is everyone all right?" coughed Badger.

"Fine," replied Rabbit. "Except Fox is squashing me!"

"And we're stuck down a hole!" snapped Fox.

"We're going to miss the stars!" sniffed one baby mouse.

"We'll find a way out," Badger said. "Don't worry."

Rabbit and Mouse sang
songs with the babies
as the others looked
for a way out.

"I've found another tunnel!"
Little Hedgehog cried.

They climbed out into
the fresh, night air and
ran to the top of
the hill at last.

High above, the sky glittered
with shooting stars.

“We made it!” laughed
Little Hedgehog. “What a night!”

And together the friends gazed
happily at the sparkly sky which
stretched on and on forever . . .

Look out for more *amazing* reads from Little Tiger Press!

For information regarding any of the above titles
or for our catalogue, please contact us:
Little Tiger Press, 1 The Coda Centre,
189 Munster Road, London SW6 6AW
Tel: 020 7385 6333
Fax: 020 7385 7333
E-mail: info@littletiger.co.uk
www.littletiger.co.uk